This Book Belongs To:

Susan Greig

CONTENTS

The Gemlin Kingdom .... Endpaper
Rupert and Pong Ping 4
Rupert and the Umbrella Boy 22
Rupert's Horse Head Paperfold 45
Rupert and the Gemlins 46
Rupert and the Snow Puzzle 64
Rupert and the Red Box 78
Rupert's Memory Test 92

ISBN 0-85079-120-0

RUPERT

A DAILY EXPRESS PUBLICATION

RUPERT

"That's Pong Ping sitting over there. And crying, too!" says Rupert Bear.

Rupert is strolling through a field near Nutwood one day when he spies his chum Pong Ping, the little Peke, sitting on a fence, looking very glum. As he gets nearer he sees that Pong Ping has been crying, which is not like him. "I say, what's up?" Rupert asks. "Oh, I'm so very homesick," the Peke sniffs. "But *this* is your home," says Rupert. "Not always," replies Pong Ping. "Climb up here and I'll explain."

and PONG PING

"Why, what's the matter?" Rupert cries.
"I'm homesick," poor Pong Ping replies.

Pong Ping's medallion makes him ache
A journey to his home to take.

"I was born in a far-off land where my father was the Emperor's favourite," Pong Ping begins and at the same time produces a medallion. "The Emperor gave him this badge and I wear it in memory of him. How I wish I could go back for a visit." "It *is* difficult, isn't it," Rupert murmurs. Then he has an idea. "Let's ask the Professor!" he exclaims. And a moment later the chums are hurrying towards their old friend's tower house.

"The old Professor's sure to know
Some way or other you may go!"

5

RUPERT'S FRIEND MAKES A CALL

"This medal's from too far away
For me to send you, I must say."

"My radio room is close at hand.
We'll try to speak to that far land."

The old man twirls the knobs around,
And presently they hear a sound.

Alas, the words don't mean a thing.
"I'll understand them," cries Pong Ping.

"First we must find out where your far-off land is," the Professor says when he hears Pong Ping's problem. "Your medal may give us a clue." And he studies the medallion closely then takes down book after book and pores through them. "Got it!" he cries at last. "This medal comes from a land deep in the Far, Far East. I can't *send* you there. But perhaps I can get a message through for you." Next moment Rupert and Pong Ping find themselves in the Professor's very own radio room.

The chums have never seen anything like it, and they gaze, open-mouthed, as the Professor twiddles and tunes and turns knobs and dials. At last he nods and puts on a pair of earphones. "Nutwood calling!" he repeats into the microphone then listens hard. He frowns and shakes his head. "I've got through, all right. But I can't understand a word they're saying." "Let me try!" Pong Ping cries. "I speak the language of that country." And the Peke jumps up and down in excitement.

RUPERT KEEPS A LOOKOUT

So Pong Ping stands upon a chair
And listens in with special care.

"The Emperor spoke!" he cries with glee,
"And said, 'Please come and stay with me'."

They think the Emperor's sure to send
His fastest 'plane to fetch his friend.

So Rupert watches from a crag
While Pong Ping goes to pack his bag.

At once the Professor gives Pong Ping the earphones and stands him on a chair in front of the microphone. Rupert watches his friend getting more and more excited as by turn he listens and talks in a language that the little bear does not understand. When Pong Ping at last jumps down from the chair he does a little dance of joy. "I've spoken to the Emperor himself," he shouts in glee. "And what do you think? He's going to send for me to go on a visit to him!"

The two chums thank the old Professor for his help and dash excitedly back to Nutwood. "The Emperor didn't say how he was going to send for me," pants Pong Ping, "but for such a long journey it surely must be by airplane!" Rupert is happy for his pal and he says, "You go and pack your things and I'll keep watch." Rupert hurries home, explains what is happening, begs some sandwiches and lemonade from Mrs. Bear then makes his way to a hillside that faces east and starts his lookout.

RUPERT GETS A SCARE

One day while Rupert's looking out,
The hill begins to shake about.

The trees shake too, the squirrels flee,
And Rupert runs, fast as can be.

And then there bursts with frightful sound,
A metal monster through the ground.

Frightened, poor Rupert runs to hide,
As from the monster two men stride.

Rupert waits and watches all afternoon but there is no sign of any airplane. Next day and the day after that, he and Pong Ping take turns at keeping watch. Then just when Rupert thinks nothing is ever going to appear, the hillside starts to shake. As rocks begin to fall Rupert jumps up and dashes towards home. To his horror the earthquake seems to be everywhere and he sees little animals fleeing in terror. "This is awful," pants poor Rupert as he runs. "What can be happening?"

Every second the earthquake gets worse with the ground shaking and trembling. Then the ground just behind Rupert heaves and pitches him on to his face. Thoroughly frightened, he scrambles behind a rock and looks back. And gasps! For, from a hole in the earth has crawled out the most strange machine. It has great claw wheels and a spinning nose for boring through the earth. Then to his amazement, a door opens and two foreign-looking men climb out.

8

RUPERT FETCHES PONG PING

Around their necks hang shiny things;
Medallions just like Pong Ping's.

"You're from the Emperor!" Rupert cries.
"I'll fetch Pong Ping", and off he flies.

"Your friends," shouts Rupert to his chum,
"By some strange kind of tank have come!"

Then off to greet them Pong Ping hies.
"So glad to see you, friends!" he cries

Hoping he has not been spotted, Rupert hides behind a tree. But the two strangers have seen him and run straight to where he is hiding. At once they start to talk very fast. Poor Rupert can't understand a word they say, then all at once he spots that both are wearing round their necks medallions like Pong Ping's. "Why, of course, you're the Emperor's messengers!" he exclaims happily. Then, making signs that he will return soon, he runs to find Pong Ping.

Rupert doesn't have far to go, for Pong Ping has come out to see what all the noise and shaking is about. "Quick!" shouts Rupert, "your friends from the Emperor are here! They didn't come by airplane after all. They were in a sort of tank thing that goes under the ground!" At first Pong Ping can't understand what Rupert is talking about, but then he spots the strangers and rushes towards them, chattering excitedly. "Oh, I do wish I knew what they were saying," thinks Rupert.

RUPERT GETS A SURPRISE TRIP

A ride for Rupert is proposed.
They jump in and the door is closed.

The strange machine with mighty roar,
Descends into the earth once more.

At length they reach a distant land
With mountains very steep and grand.

"We leave you now," the two men say.
"You cross that bridge to find your way."

Pong Ping turns to Rupert. "You're quite right," he says. "They are from the Emperor and they've come to take me to him. But let's have a joyride first, shall we?" "Rather!" cries Rupert. So they scramble in and shut the door. But at once the machine plunges back into the hole from which it came. Rupert shouts at the driver to turn back but he doesn't understand. Then he turns to Pong Ping who is smiling mischievously. "I told him to do that," says the Peke. "I want you to come with me on holiday! Sorry, Rupert, but I do like to have someone with me and I'm sure you'll like it." "Oh, well—," Rupert agrees. But he still finds the journey through the earth long and dark and he is relieved when they emerge beside a river. After Pong Ping and the two men have spoken together, the little Peke says, "They say we must make our own way from here. They've told me what we must do. They say that first we have to make for that bridge over there. So let's go."

RUPERT SUMMONS THE BIRDS

They cross the bridge named by their guide,
And come upon a mountain side.

And there they see, as they were told,
A trumpet that is plainly old.

The trumpet's notes sound loud and clear.
And now two splendid birds appear.

"Come, scramble on our backs," they cry.
They stretch their wings and off they fly.

The bridge, when they come to it, is very steep and seems to lead nowhere but the steep sides of a high mountain. But Pong Ping doesn't hesitate. He leads the way upward until at last he stops and points to a crevice in the rock. Rupert can just make out a kind of trumpet. "That's what I was told to look for," says Pong Ping. "We have to blow it. Since you're stronger than I am you'd better do the blowing." Mystified, Rupert climbs up and takes the strange instrument.

He puts the trumpet to his lips and blows. To his delight it makes a loud, beautiful sound. Almost at once, in answer to the call, two great birds appear from beyond the mountain and fly towards the chums. "Climb on to our backs and hold tight!" they cry as they land. That is a lot easier said than done because their feathers are so smooth, but at length the pals are in position. "Off we go!" cry the birds, and with that launch themselves into space.

11

RUPERT MEETS THE EMPEROR

They cross a mighty mountain range
To reach a palace rich and strange.

An armoured soldier halts the pair,
And fixes them with frightening stare.

Pong Ping displays his medal rare.
The man at once admits the pair.

Then to the Emperor's room they're shown,
And find him seated on a throne.

High over the mountains fly the great birds with Rupert and Pong Ping clinging to their backs. At first Rupert can hardly bear to open his eyes but when he does so he sees a magnificent city below. Its buildings have spiky roofs and bright-coloured walls. "The Emperor's secret city," says the bird as it descends. The two birds put the pals down on a sort of terrace. Just as Rupert is wondering what happens next a fierce-looking soldier appears and says something Rupert doesn't understand.

Pong Ping, though, seems to understand for he produces his medallion and shows it to the soldier. The man studies the medallion and when he hands it back to Pong Ping he is much more respectful. Beckoning the pals to follow, he leads the way to a very large room where a friendly-looking man is seated on a throne. "The Emperor!" gasps Pong Ping. "Oh, and that must be his pet dragon." Just then the Emperor smiles and beckons to them to approach.

RUPERT IS GIVEN A WARNING

At supper Rupert's in a fix;
He finds he has to use chopsticks.

A hissing startles Rupert Bear.
He turns. A dragon's lurking there!

The dragon shouts, "It is a shame!
I've been neglected since you came!"

"My dreaded uncle flying there
Will carry off your friend, young bear."

"My old favourite's son! Welcome, welcome!" cries the Emperor. And Rupert is delighted to hear the kindly ruler speak a language that he understands. "Well, you must be hungry after your long journey," the Emperor goes on, and almost at once the friends find themselves at a table with a wonderful meal in front of them. Rupert, though, does have a bit of trouble with his chopsticks at first. Later when they set out to tour the palace, Rupert, who is lagging behind, hears a hiss from a corner and turns to find the Emperor's pet dragon. To his horror it grabs him by the scruff of the neck and drags him out on to a wide terrace. "Listen," it hisses. "I was the Emperor's favourite till your friend came. Tell him to go back at once or my uncle, the Flying Dragon, will put an end to him—understand?" He points towards the sky and there Rupert sees the sinister form of the great Flying Dragon.

RUPERT'S PAL IS CARRIED OFF

That night when both are fast asleep,
The dragon towards them starts to creep.

Rupert is wakened by a squeak.
The dragon's got his pal, the Peke.

Then to the Emperor Rupert goes
And tells of Pong Ping's dragon foes.

"To you a travel-bird I'll lend
To help you find your little friend."

To Rupert's astonishment Pong Ping is not at all worried by the dragon's threat. "I am the Emperor's favourite," he says. "No one would dare touch me." But Rupert is still uneasy as they settle down to sleep that night. After their long journey the chums are so tired and sleep so soundly that neither sees the frightening figure that glares through their window just as dawn is breaking. It is a cry of fear that wakens Rupert who opens his eyes to see his chum being hauled through the window by a great scaly claw. "The Flying Dragon!" he cries and, leaping from bed, dashes to the Emperor's chamber to tell him. But to his dismay the Emperor does nothing but moan, "Oh, dear, the Flying Dragon! No one can do anything about that, I fear!" "Oh, please let *me* try to rescue Pong Ping!" cries Rupert. "Oh, well, if you like," says the Emperor helplessly. "I shall send you on a travel-bird after them." And he has a bird summoned.

14

RUPERT MEETS THE WISE WOMAN

The bird says, "To a cave we'll go.
A wise old woman's there, I know."

"And to her words you must give heed.
Without her help you can't succeed."

The wise old woman hears his tale
And says, "Your courage must prevail."

"This drink will make the dragon sleep
For many hours in slumber deep."

As Rupert climbs aboard the bird the Emperor says, "The bird will take you close to the lair of the Flying Dragon. But, oh dear, it is a most dangerous task you have taken on. Good luck!" The bird heads deep into the mountains where at last it sets Rupert down on a high rock. "On your own you can never get Pong Ping back," it says. "But in that cave down there lives a wise old woman. Ask her advice. If she won't help you then you will never succeed. I shall wait here for you." Rupert scrambles down to the cave and just inside it comes upon the wise old woman. She nods as he pours out his story. "You are a person of great courage, otherwise you would not have got so far," she says. Then, handing Rupert a flask, she goes on, "This is a secret mixture. Somehow you must get the Flying Dragon to drink it. If he does he will sleep for half a day and only then you may be able to rescue your friend. But it will not be easy. Good luck!"

RUPERT TRIES A TRICK

The bird takes Rupert all the way,
And says, "I'll call here every day."

The dragon's eating from a tree,
But no Pong Ping can Rupert see.

"He never drinks," a lizard cries.
"You'll have to catch him otherwise."

"Because the drinking plan's no use,
I'll paint the dragon's tree with juice."

Rupert scrambles back to the bird which carries him the rest of the way to the lair of the Flying Dragon, a deep valley. "You must go on alone," it says. "Each evening two of us birds will return here in case you rescue your friend. Good luck!" And off it flies. So Rupert makes his way into the valley until a munching noise stops him. He edges forward and, peeping from behind a rock, sees the dragon eating the top branches of a tree. "How can I get it to drink the sleeping mixture?" Rupert wonders aloud. "He doesn't drink anything for fear of putting out the fire he breathes," pipes up a little voice. Rupert turns to see a very small lizard. "None of us here likes the Flying Dragon," it goes on. "So I'll tell you that your only hope is to paint the leaves of one of his food trees with your mixture." It points out a good tree and Rupert sets to, using his scarf to paint all its leaves with the sleeping mixture.

RUPERT'S TRICK WORKS

"My trick's worked!" Rupert cries in glee.
"The dragon's eaten all the tree!"

He finds the dragon lying still.
Can he the rescue now fulfil?

Towards the giant beast he creeps
To make quite sure the dragon sleeps.

But when in vain he hunts about,
He says, "I'll have to risk a shout."

When he has painted all the leaves Rupert finds a safe spot and settles down for the night. It is daylight when he wakens and once more he steals down into the valley. To his delight he finds that the Flying Dragon must have returned during the night and eaten up all of the tree. "After gobbling down all that sleeping mixture it can't have got far," he thinks and sets out to explore. And, sure enough, he soon comes across the tail of the dragon. The rest of it is hidden behind a rock. But is it asleep? Holding his breath, he peeps round the rock. Ah! The dragon is fast asleep and gently breathing fire. "Whew!" Rupert lets out a sigh. Now to find Pong Ping. Keeping as quiet as he can, Rupert hunts among the rocks, but no trace of his pal can he find. "I'll just have to shout for him and risk wakening the dragon," he decides. He climbs on to a rock a little way from the dragon and shouts, "Pong Ping! It's me—Rupert! Where are you?"

RUPERT RESCUES PONG PING

When Rupert turns, his foe still sleeps,
But round a boulder Pong Ping peeps.

He says, to still poor Pong Ping's fright,
"The birds will meet us here tonight."

"Well done, brave bear!" the Emperor cries.
"My golden medal is your prize."

But now a courtier cries with fear,
"Oh, sire, these two must not stay here."

A slight noise from where the dragon lies asleep makes Rupert start and swing round. To his great relief the beast is still slumbering, and peeping from behind a nearby rock is Pong Ping, still in his pyjamas. In hurried whispers Rupert explains about the sleeping mixture. "But we must hurry before the mixture stops working!" he declares, and taking Pong Ping by the hand, leads him up the steep side of the valley to where the birds have arranged to come each evening. As they reach the spot two travel-birds appear and very soon the pals are flying back to the Emperor's palace which they reach as dawn is breaking. The kindly old ruler is delighted at Pong Ping's rescue and orders that Rupert be awarded a golden medal for his bravery. But the rejoicing does not last long. No sooner is Pong Ping properly dressed again than an aged courtier appears. "Majesty," he quavers, "these two must not stay here. Come, I shall show you the reason why."

18

RUPERT AND PONG PING FLEE

The courtier points towards the sky,
And there they see the dragon fly.

The chums are hurried out of sight
For fear of that fierce dragon's spite.

The Emperor says, "I can't, you see,
Keep you two longer here with me."

So down the cellar chute they slide;
A steep and dark and bumpy ride.

The old courtier leads the way on to the terrace and points at the sky. "There!" he cries. "The Flying Dragon! Awake once more and I am quite sure looking for its escaped captive. If he finds Pong Ping here he will breathe fire upon us in his anger and burn us all up!" "Oh, dear! Gracious me!" gasps the Emperor who, though kind, is not at all brave. "We'd better get them away." And at once a guard is summoned and told to take the two chums out of sight. The burly guard picks up Rupert and Pong Ping and, followed by the Emperor, hurries them deep into the palace cellars. He sets them down on two mats at the edge of a hole in the floor. "Sorry about this," the Emperor says. "Come again when things are a bit quieter." "Thank you," Pong Ping replies. "I should love it if things really *were* a bit quieter." The Emperor nods. The guard gives the chums a push—and then suddenly they are sliding downwards through the earth in pitch darkness.

RUPERT REACHES THE PLAIN

When they are nearly in despair
They shoot into the open air.

And Rupert gives a happy shout,
"It was from here we started out!"

They clamber down towards the plain
And see their driver once again.

And then a bird towards them flies.
"It brings a message," Rupert cries.

Faster and faster the chums slide down the steep, dark slope. Then suddenly the slope is not so steep, there is daylight ahead and they swish into the open where a smooth rock checks their speed and prevents their being dashed on to the boulders below. Gazing around, Rupert exclaims, "I know where we are! This is where we started from before we called the birds." And so very carefully the two chums climb down over the boulders to the river. They cross the steep bridge again and start across the plain. "See! There's the tank thing that brought us here!" Rupert cries. Just then the driver of the tank spies the pals and runs to them. To Rupert's surprise he finds himself grabbed by the man who chatters sternly at them. "He says we should still be at the palace," explains Pong Ping. "He has had no orders about us." But at that moment Rupert spies one of the Emperor's travel-birds with something in its beak.

RUPERT IS SAFELY HOME

"The Emperor's orders," says the bird.
The driver reads the royal word.

Then in his arms the chums he takes
And for the tank he quickly makes.

Loud rumbling gives the Bears a fright,
And then the tank comes into sight.

"You see this hole?" says Rupert Bear.
"We've been to Pong Ping's land down there."

The great bird lands beside the driver who takes a scroll from its beak, unrolls it and reads. "That's the Emperor's orders about you," the bird explains. "I tried to get here first but you travelled so fast I was left behind." The driver finishes reading and without a word he lifts the chums and hurries to the tank. "I think we're going home," gasps Rupert. "I hope so!" Pong Ping says. "I shall never be homesick for this part of the world again."

Sometime later, back in Nutwood, Rupert's Mummy and Daddy, who are on their way to ask the police if anything has been seen of Rupert, suddenly hear a rumbling and find themselves face to face with a strange machine. In another moment Rupert and Pong Ping have jumped out, the machine has bored its way back into the earth and Mr. and Mrs. Bear are peering, amazed, down the hole that goes to the Far, Far East. "I'll tell you all about it over supper!" laughs Rupert.

21

A strange pedlar vows revenge when Mr. Bear refuses to buy his wares. As a result Rupert finds himself in danger.

RUPERT MEETS THE PEDLAR

How Rupert and his Daddy stare
To find a pedlar standing there.

The pedlar man will not take "No!",
And all his wares proceeds to show.

Rupert is helping his Daddy in the garden one day when they hear the front gate squeak. They look up to see a strangely-dressed man standing there. Plainly he is a pedlar of some sort for he is heavily laden with rugs and trinkets and bundles. There is something about the man that makes Rupert feel uneasy. His wide smile looks false and, without waiting to be asked, he comes right into the garden. He puts down his bundles and begins to undo them. "No, please, we really don't want anything ..." Mr. Bear begins politely. The man acts as if he has not heard and goes on unwrapping his bundles and laying out his wares on the grass. All the time he is doing this he smiles his big, false smile and pays no attention to Mr. Bear's efforts to stop him. At last he straightens up, holding out a flask. "Lovely things. You buy, eh?" he says.

UMBRELLA BOY

RUPERT'S DADDY WILL NOT BUY

Though Mr. Bear says, "Not today",
The man goes on with his display.

The angry pedlar turns to glare
And wave his fist at Mr. Bear.

"Please, you must understand, we don't want to buy anything today, thank you," Mr. Bear repeats patiently. But the stranger will not listen and begins to display more and more of his wares. "Lovely carpets? Shawls? Silks from far-away lands? You buy?" he wheedles. "Very cheap. Good bargains. I come long way to bring you these beautiful things. Come on, you buy, eh?" And the smile is fixed on his face all the time. But

it disappears when at long last he accepts that Mr. Bear really isn't going to buy any of his goods. Angrily he bundles up his things and as he does so he mutters to himself. He is still muttering as he stamps out of the garden. At the gate he turns, glares at Rupert and Mr. Bear and brandishes a fist. "What a nasty man," says Mr. Bear. "Yes," thinks Rupert. "And I just hope we've seen the last of him."

RUPERT FINDS THE BOY

Rupert watches the man depart
With all his wares piled in a cart.

Rupert, as he jogs along,
Sees Sara—and there's something wrong!

"Oh, Rupert, do please come and see.
There's someone ill beside a tree."

A strange boy sits upon the ground,
Umbrellas scattered all around.

Mrs. Bear has been watching through the window and when the stranger has gone she calls Rupert and sends him on an errand to the greengrocer's. "And when you go have a look round and make sure that pedlar has gone," Mr. Bear adds. "I didn't much like the look of him." From the garden gate Rupert sees the man trundling his wares away in a wheelbarrow. He watches him out of sight then heads for the village. On the way he sees someone running towards him. It is his friend Sara, but she looks as if something is wrong. "I say, what's up?" Rupert greets her. Sara catches her breath. "I was on my way to get something for my Mummy," she pants, "but I've found someone who seems to be in trouble. Come and see." And she leads Rupert back to where a dark-skinned boy is seated under a tree. He seems to be fast asleep for he does not stir when the chums run up. Scattered round him are a number of umbrellas made of thick, brightly coloured paper.

RUPERT TAKES THE BOY HOME

The boy starts up and cries, "Buy, please!"
He's like the pedlar, Rupert sees.

As Rupert thinks, "Why's he alone?"
The boy collapses with a moan.

The boy feels weak, and so he should,
With too much work and little food.

Says Rupert kindly, "Come with me.
Mummy's the one that you should see."

Rupert is just starting to whisper, "I wonder what's wrong with him" when the boy starts awake. His eyes open wide in alarm and he jumps up. As he does so he snatches up some of the umbrellas and holds one out. "Nice umbrella. You buy, eh?" he pleads. "Why, he talks like that pedlar," Rupert realises. "And he's wearing the same sort of clothes. I wonder if they're father and son." He is just about to tell Sara of the pedlar when the boy collapses with a little moan.

Rupert starts forward and helps the boy to his feet. "Are you ill?" he asks anxiously. "Would you like me to find the pedlar man? He is your father, isn't he?" "No, not my father," the boy says shakily. "He is my master. Makes me sell umbrellas all day. Much work but not much food." "Then you're coming to see my Mummy," Rupert says firmly. And with Sara carrying the boy's umbrellas, Rupert leads the young stranger gently back to the Bear family's cottage.

RUPERT'S MUMMY FEEDS THE BOY

"A rest, poor boy, will do you good,
And so will this hot drink and food."

Now on her errand Sara goes.
The boy is in good hands, she knows.

The boy must now be on his way.
His master's cross. He dare not stay.

"Though made of paper it's quite strong.
This umbrella will serve you long."

When Mrs. Bear hears about the boy she bustles about getting food and drink for him. Soon the little stranger is tucking in and beginning to look better. When he has finished he thanks Mrs. Bear and the chums, then goes on to explain what he is doing in Nutwood. He has to trudge round after his master, the pedlar, trying to sell umbrellas. If he can't sell any he gets no pay and very little food. Now the boy is feeling better Sara says she must get on with the errand for her Mummy. "You needn't hurry off," Mrs. Bear tells the boy. "Rest a while." But in a very short while the boy is on his feet again. "Must go or my master will be angry," he sighs. "Must try to sell my umbrellas." "May I see one of your umbrellas?" asks Mrs. Bear. "Why, it is pretty," she says when she opens one. "Yes, and though it is made of paper it is very strong and will last a long time," says the boy. "Then I shall buy one," smiles Rupert's Mummy.

RUPERT FINDS AN UMBRELLA

"My master's bad man, little bear.
You and your family must take care."

The poor boy trudges off to find
His master who is so unkind.

Thinks Rupert, "Poor umbrella boy.
I wish that we could bring him joy."

"That's funny," thinks the little bear.
"Sara left no umbrella there."

The boy is overjoyed that Mrs. Bear has bought one of his umbrellas and he is much more cheerful when Rupert shows him to the gate. But before he goes he pauses and asks, "Did you buy anything from my master when he came?" When he hears how Mr. Bear sent the man packing he looks solemn. "Oh dear," he says. "My master will be very angry. Maybe even he will put bad spell on your nice family. Please, little bear, be very careful." And he hurries off after his master.

Wishing that he could do something to make the umbrella boy's life happier, Rupert sets off once more on his errand to the greengrocer's. He hasn't gone far, though, when he sees an umbrella propped against a tree. "Now, how did that get there?" he wonders. "I'm sure Sara didn't leave any behind when we took the boy home. She brought away all the umbrellas that were scattered around where he had been sitting. What's more the boy didn't say anything about missing one."

27

RUPERT TAKES SHELTER

"If Sara didn't leave it here,
The pedlar must have done, I fear."

"I'll hide it here until I may
Return it later on today."

Then all at once the rainstorm breaks.
For shelter Rupert quickly makes.

He crouches by the garden gate
And hopes the storm will soon abate.

Rupert examines the umbrella. "Yes, it's just the same as the others. But I'm quite sure *we* didn't leave it here. So who did? And why was it propped carefully against a tree so that it was bound to be seen? The boy's master must have done it while the boy was in our garden. I wonder why." Rupert ponders a moment then decides to hide the umbrella in the bushes and return it to the boy when he has run his errand. He carefully notes the spot then hurries on his way.

Before Rupert has gone very far a great wind springs up, the sky darkens and heavy rain teems down. "I must find some shelter!" Rupert gasps. "Ah, there's Mrs. Sheep's cottage. I can shelter behind her thick hedge." He dashes for the gate and huddles beside the hedge there. "Oh, that's better!" he pants. "This hedge is so thick it keeps both the rain and the wind off me. I'll stay here until the worst of the storm passes. It shouldn't be long."

RUPERT KNOWS WHO'S TO BLAME

He thinks that he is on his own
Until he hears a little moan.

Then through the gate he takes a peep
And sees that it's old Mrs. Sheep.

"My best shrub's looking such a fright!
An hour ago it was all right."

Says Mrs. Sheep, "A pedlar came."
Now Rupert's certain who's to blame.

At last the rain eases off and Rupert is just about to go when he notices that old Mrs. Sheep has come out of her cottage and is making small moaning noises. Rupert pushes open the gate and asks, "Is something wrong?" "Just look!" says Mrs. Sheep. She points to a shrub in a big pot. It is burned and shrivelled. "It was my best one," she says. "Just an hour ago it was all right." "Has anyone been here in that hour?" asks Rupert. "Only a pedlar and a boy selling umbrellas," replies Mrs. Sheep. "Then I think I know what has happened," Rupert says quietly and he tells Mrs. Sheep about the umbrella boy: "He is a sort of slave to the man and he told me that his master is a bad man who can do magic and sometimes puts a spell on those who won't buy his things. *He* must have killed your plant. But I mustn't wait. I'm on an errand for my Mummy and I'm awfully late already." So, saying goodbye, Rupert hurries away towards Nutwood.

RUPERT HEARS OF A MYSTERY

"I wonder," thinks the little bear,
"What Tigerlily's doing there."

The little girl tells Rupert there
Is something mystic in the air.

"Whenever that strange magic's near
This spark will on my wand appear."

Cries Rupert, "I believe I know
Who's caused the magic. Please don't go!"

Just outside Nutwood village Rupert catches up with a friend who is looking unusually thoughtful. It is Tigerlily, the Chinese Conjurer's daughter. "Hello, what are you doing out here?" Rupert greets her. "I am helping my honourable Daddy", Tigerlily replies mysteriously. "With that wand?" Rupert asks. Tigerlily considers for a moment then seems to make up her mind. "Perhaps I shall tell you, yes," she says. She gazes at Rupert for a moment then whispers, "Something mysterious in the air!"

Tigerlily sits down and explains. "My Daddy is very worried. He can feel magic in the air that is different from his magic. He is too busy to look for it so he sends me. Ah, there, see!" And she points to a spark which has appeared at the tip of her wand. "Strange magic do that ... but now it is gone again. What can it be?" "The pedlar!" exclaims Rupert jumping up. "He can make magic spells! Oh, just wait till I've run my errand, Tigerlily, and I'll explain!"

RUPERT MEETS SARA AGAIN

Now, having done his shopping chore,
Young Rupert battles back once more.

Though Tigerlily he can't see,
There's Sara sheltering by a tree.

"This odd umbrella I found here.
There's something not quite right, I fear."

"Still, since it's coming on to rain,
You use it till it's fair again."

Rupert dashes into the village, buys what Mrs. Bear wants, then starts back to where he left Tigerlily. As he battles against the wind which has sprung up again, stronger than ever, he tells himself, "I'm sure that pedlar's the answer to Tigerlily's mystery." But when he reaches the spot where he left her he can find no sign of the girl. Puzzled and rather worried, he pushes on towards home. On the way he comes across Sara sheltering from the gale behind a tree. "I'm on my way back from my Mummy's errand," she explains. "I met the umbrella boy again and he feels much better thanks to your Mummy. But, oh, Rupert, he still isn't really happy!" She sees why when Rupert tells her what he has learned about the boy and his harsh master. He tells her, too, about the other umbrella he has found and shows her where he hid it. Just then it starts to rain. "Here, Sara, you use the umbrella to get home," Rupert says. "We can return it later to the boy."

RUPERT HEARS ALARMING NEWS

"I must get home. I'm very late,"
Thinks Rupert, but a voice cries, "Wait!"

He wants to know if Rupert's found
A strange umbrella lying 'round.

"On that umbrella," says the lad,
"My master's cast a spell that's bad."

"You look for Sara on this track.
I'll take this home and hurry back."

Sara turns for home delighted with the umbrella. Rupert calls after her, "It's awfully light so do hold it tight in this strong wind." "Of course, I shall," Sara shouts back and off she goes. "Well, I better push on home, rain or no rain," Rupert says to himself. "I've been so long on this errand Mummy will think I've got lost." But as he is hurrying along a shout makes him turn, and there is the umbrella boy. He looks troubled. "Please, have you found another umbrella?" he asks.

"Why, yes, as a matter of fact I did," Rupert replies. "And I must say it had me puzzled for I was quite sure we hadn't left any behind when we took you home." "Oh, no, *I* did not leave it!" cries the boy. "My master put it there for you to find. He has put a spell on it. A very bad spell. You must not touch!" "Oh, my goodness!" Rupert exclaims. "And I've given it to Sara! You go after her. She went that way. I must take this shopping home. I'll be back very soon!"

RUPERT HURRIES BACK TO HELP

Rupert tells Mummy of the plan
To spite them by the pedlar man.

Says Rupert, "Please don't be alarmed.
Your umbrella has not been harmed."

"Be careful, dear," says Mrs. Bear.
"If there's bad magic in the air."

"Something is wrong," thinks Rupert when
He comes upon the boy again.

"Dear me, you've been a long time," Mrs. Bear greets Rupert. "Did you have to shelter from the rain?" "Oh, it wasn't really the rain that held me up," Rupert explains. "I found another umbrella, you see, and I lent it to Sara when she was caught in the rain. Then the umbrella boy found me and said his master had put a spell on it and that it was dangerous ..." "Oh, dear!" Mrs. Bear exclaims. "And I bought an umbrella, too!" "Yours is all right," says Rupert. "But Sara may be in trouble." Rupert's Mummy wants him to come indoors and have something to eat, but the little bear pleads, "Not just yet, please! I promised the umbrella boy I'd help him to find Sara and warn her." Mrs. Bear isn't happy about Rupert's going where there might be bad magic, but she lets him go with a warning to be very, very careful. Off Rupert hurries to where he left the boy. Before he gets there he sees the boy hurrying towards him, waving urgently.

RUPERT'S PAL IS IN DANGER

"Oh, come and see please, little bear!
Your friend's been swept up in the air."

And Rupert's heart sinks when he sees
Poor Sara high above the trees.

The boy says, "This bad spell I know.
When she gets tired she will let go!"

"Come back!" he hears the strange boy shout,
And wonders what it's all about.

"Oh, come quick, little bear!" gasps the boy as he dashes up. "Just like I warned you. Magic in umbrella very bad. Your friend Sara, she is going up, far away ..." "I don't understand!" Rupert interrupts. "What's happened to Sara?" "No time!" cries the boy. "Oh, please come and see!" He pulls Rupert to the top of a slope and points to something being blown along above the trees. "It's Sara!" gasps Rupert. "And she's hanging on to the umbrella. Oh, how awful! Come on, we mustn't lose sight of her!" Off the two dash and as they run the umbrella boy pants, "I have seen this spell before. My master puts it on umbrella handle. When handle gets warm then magic works. It goes up in air. Sara frightened to let go. But soon she must tire and ..." Rupert is so horrified at what the boy has told him that he puts on a spurt and dashes ahead. But he really isn't watching where he is going and he is brought up short by a shout from the boy.

RUPERT FINDS SARA

The umbrella is floating free.
No sign of Sara can they see.

"She must be hurt!" cries Rupert Bear.
"Come on, we must search everywhere."

Then as the two friends search about
From high above they hear a shout.

"If," Rupert says, "you'll just help me,
I know that I can climb this tree."

Rupert finds that in his anxiety to catch up with Sara he has run into a thick wood. The boy is calling and beckoning him to come back to the clearing where he is hopping about in excitement and pointing upwards. When Rupert reaches him and looks up at the sky he gives a groan of horror. The umbrella is in sight above the trees but there is no sign of Sara. "Oh, how awful!" he cries. "She must have fallen. She's probably badly hurt. Come on, we must search everywhere!"

The two hurry to the trees over which they last saw Sara. "It's most likely she fell around here somewhere," Rupert pants as they enter the wood. "Let's both call her. She may be able to answer. Sara! Sara! It's Rupert! Shout if you can hear me!" And almost at once comes an answering cry, "Up here, Rupert!" "Goodness, she's caught in a tree!" Rupert exclaims with relief. "It's this one. I say, give me a hand up," he calls to the boy. "I'll climb up and get her."

RUPERT RESCUES HIS CHUM

"Now, Sara, follow me and then
We'll soon be safely down again."

The two pals quickly reach the ground,
Thanks to Rupert, safe and sound.

"This boy," says Rupert, "told me why
You were whisked up into the sky."

"We have no time to stand around.
That bad umbrella must be found!"

Rupert, who is very good at climbing, soon shins up the tree. And there, among the top branches, he sees Sara. She is still shaken and frightened but to Rupert's delight she is unharmed. "Now, I'll lead the way down," Rupert tells her. "Just do as I do and you'll be fine." Down they go and when they reach the lower branches Sara begins to tell what happened to her: "Quite suddenly the umbrella lifted me off my feet. It was so quick that I daren't let go. When we hit the top of this tree I grabbed the branches and just let the wretched umbrella go." "When we get down I shall tell you why it all happened," Rupert promises as they reach the ground. The umbrella boy is plainly happy to see that they are safe. "This boy has told me that his wicked uncle put a magic spell on the umbrella because we didn't buy anything from him," Rupert tells Sara. "It was really meant for me." "Now I must find that umbrella," the boy says and turns away. "Let's help him," says Sara.

RUPERT TELLS TIGERLILY

The pals call to him, "We'll help you!"
Then Tigerlily comes in view.

"This boy knows," says the little bear,
"Why there's strange magic in the air."

"I point my magic-finder, so,
And any strange spells make it glow."

"I must tell Daddy what you say,"
Says Rupert's chum and darts away.

Rupert and Sara set off after the umbrella boy who plainly wants to find the troublesome umbrella before it can do any more harm. Then Rupert spies a familiar figure. "Hey, stop!" he shouts after the boy. "Here's Tigerlily. She'll want to know all about this." The boy turns back and he and the Chinese Conjurer's daughter gaze curiously at each other. "This boy knows all about the magic that I'm sure interfered with your Daddy's magic," Rupert begins. "Magic? You do magic?" the boy asks in surprise. Tigerlily smiles and explains about her Daddy and how he has sent her to find out about the strange magic. "It is still here, this other magic," she says and moves her wand about until a spark appears at its tip. "Hey, I have an idea!" exclaims Rupert. "That spark could be caused by the magic umbrella we're looking for. You may have been pointing at it." At once Tigerlily is serious. "I must fetch my Daddy," she says and hurries off home.

37

RUPERT AND HIS CHUMS HIDE

"Quick, hide!" cries Sara as she sees
The pedlar coming through the trees.

Then all three scurry off to find
A tree or bush to hide behind.

The man's so near Rupert's aghast,
But luckily he hurries past.

When he comes out, the little bear
Can't see his two pals anywhere.

"I still think I may be right about the cause of the spark on Tigerlily's wand," Rupert says. "Come on, let's see if we can remember which way she was pointing it at the time. We may find the magic umbrella." But before they can start, the boy, who has been looking around, gives a warning hiss. Sara follows his frightened gaze. "Look out!" she whispers. "There's a man coming. I'm sure it's your pedlar. Quick, hide, everyone!" And the three scatter for cover.

Peeping from behind the big tree where he has concealed himself, Rupert watches the pedlar man striding straight ahead. Clearly he does not know anyone is near. When the man has gone the little bear comes out of hiding. "Oh, dear, I didn't see where the others went to hide," he thinks. "And I daren't call in case the pedlar hears. What's the best thing to do? I know, I'll see if Tigerlily is coming back yet." And he starts towards the Conjurer's house.

RUPERT HELPS THE CONJURER

*Then up the track towards him come
Her Daddy and his Chinese chum.*

*The two are interested to hear
The pedlar man is somewhere near.*

*The arrow points. The three friends see
The umbrella is up this tree.*

*"My spell will keep you safe and so
To fetch it to me, up you go!"*

As Rupert comes in sight of the tall pagoda-like house where the Chinese Conjurer lives he sees Tigerlily and her Daddy approaching. "I have told my Daddy about other strange magic in the air," Tigerlily says. "He says he is sure it is not good magic and he comes to find out for himself." "Shall I show you where the umbrella drifted and where Sara got caught in the tree?" asks Rupert. "And, oh, the pedlar who put the spell on it is near here. I've just seen him."

"Thank you," says the Conjurer. "But I think my magic-finder can seek out this strange umbrella." He presses a switch on a machine he is carrying and the needle on top of it swings round for a moment then points steadily at a nearby tree. "I am sure umbrella is up this tree," he says. "Will you climb up and get it, Rupert? I shall surround you with good magic so that you cannot fall." And for the second time that day the little bear shins up a very tall tree.

39

RUPERT GETS A NASTY SHOCK

Then from the tree he tries to pluck
The wretched thing—Oh, dear, it's stuck!

He tugs the thing then finds that he
Is tugged by it, right off the tree!

Just when he thinks he must let go
He feels a sort of pull below.

"Someone is pulling me down there—
The pedlar!" cries the little bear.

Because he knows he can't fall, Rupert makes good speed up the tree. And there, right at the top, trapped in the branches, is the umbrella he is seeking. He stretches forward, grasps it by the handle and with his other hand reaches for the catch to close it. Then ... "Hey! What on earth's happening?" he gasps. "I can't let go of it! And it's pulling me out of the tree! Oh, the spell is still working. Help! Help!" But Rupert's cries are in vain and he is pulled clear of the tree. At once a stiff breeze sends him soaring over the forest out of sight of the Conjurer and Tigerlily. Then just when he is beginning to think he can't hold on very much longer he starts to sink. "It feels as if I'm being pulled down by something," he thinks. "I wonder if it's more of the Conjurer's magic." But when he looks down it is not the Conjurer he sees waving handkerchiefs and reciting a spell. It is the pedlar.

RUPERT IS CAPTURED

*Poor Rupert thinks, "I must be brave
And not betray the pedlar's slave."*

*"Run, Sara!" Rupert cries. "Don't wait!"
But Sara seems to hesitate.*

*The pedlar casts a spell then he
Hears someone move behind a tree.*

*The pedlar's servant has been found.
All three find they're stuck to the ground.*

Helplessly Rupert is pulled towards the ground. As soon as he is near enough to the ground to drop safely he finds that once more he cannot let go of the umbrella. Seemingly the spell allows you to let go only when it is dangerous to do so, he realises. The pedlar grabs him: "Now, little bear, you shall tell me where my servant boy has gone. The rascal has run away." Rupert makes up his mind that he will tell the man nothing and just then Sara appears. "Run for it, Sara!" the little bear shouts. Startled, Sara hesitates. The pedlar pushes Rupert towards her and with a flourish of his hand pronounces a spell. Then he darts behind a tree where he seems to have heard something and repeats the spell. "Now's our chance," whispers Rupert. But when he tries to go he can't move. Nor can Sara . . . and nor can the umbrella boy who is standing beside the tree behind which the pedlar disappeared. "So that's who he heard," Rupert says dismally.

RUPERT'S FRIENDS TURN UP

"My master's very angry man.
He's working out some nasty plan."

"What's happening?" cries the little bear,
As sparkling colours fill the air.

The startled pals are all still dazed
When back the pedlar runs, amazed.

A loud voice makes the pedlar turn.
The Conjurer stands looking stern.

"Cannot move," quavers the umbrella boy. "My master has put a spell on us. He is very angry. See, he walks away to think and plan what to do with us next." "And whatever it is," Rupert thinks, "it won't be nice." "But why am I in all this?" Sara pipes up. "I'd never even seen that man until a minute ago and I've had a bad enough fright already with that awful umbrella!" "That's why he's angry," Rupert says. "You see the umbrella was meant for me . . . hey, what's all this?" Rupert breaks off, for the air has begun to quiver and spark and crackle. The pedlar rushes back. "What is this? Do you make new magic, little girl?" he demands angrily. But before Sara can reply, a loud, stern voice makes them swing round. And there, surrounded by more crackling coloured sparks, is the Chinese Conjurer. Tigerlily is standing beside him and both are staring fixedly at the pedlar who is startled by their sudden appearance.

RUPERT AND HIS PALS ARE FREE

The chums now realise with glee
That once again their feet are free.

"Your Daddy's magic was sublime.
But it was only just in time."

The Conjurer in no time quells
The pedlar and his nasty spells.

The pedlar's told he is a knave
For making the poor boy a slave.

At last the Chinese Conjurer speaks and his voice is scornful. "So it is you who make bad magic, eh? And you put evil spells on our little Nutwood people. This I cannot allow. You will go and you will go far away and you will stay away, you wicked man!" At that moment Rupert and the others find they can move again and they rush towards Tigerlily. "I say, did your Daddy's machine find us? Did he make all those stars and things?" asks Rupert. "You were only just in time!" "Yes, yes!" cries Tigerlily. "Now my honourable Daddy put everything right." By this time the pedlar has realised that he is no match for the Conjurer and is looking scared. The Conjurer is still angry. He points to the umbrella boy. "Rupert tells me this poor boy sells umbrellas for you." His voice is stern. "He is not your son. You pay him nothing and feed him poorly. He is nothing more than a slave. That is so, yes?"

RUPERT'S NEW CHUM IS HAPPY

*"There is no slavery here and so
Far from this country you must go!"*

*"Now listen carefully, you're free
To choose your master, him or me."*

*At once the boy makes up his mind.
He picks the Conjurer, wise and kind.*

*He starts for his new home with joy,
No longer "the umbrella boy".*

For a moment the pedlar tries to bluster but he can see from the Conjurer's face that he is wasting his time. "No, you cannot deny that this poor boy is no better than a slave," the Conjurer cuts him short scornfully. Then he turns to the poor umbrella boy. "You shall choose your master," he tells him gently. "Him or me. If me, you get good living and learn good magic." The umbrella boy can hardly believe his ears. Then for the first time Rupert sees him grin. "You!" he says.

When the pedlar has been sent packing for good the Conjurer relaxes and smiles. "It was lucky for all of you that Rupert told Tigerlily about that man and his wicked spells and that she came and fetched me in time to get you out of very bad trouble. And now this boy shall be free if he wishes." But the boy, who is no longer the umbrella boy, has made up his mind to stay with the Conjurer, and off they go together. "I'm so glad for him!" laughs Rupert.

44

RUPERT'S HORSE HEAD PAPERFOLD

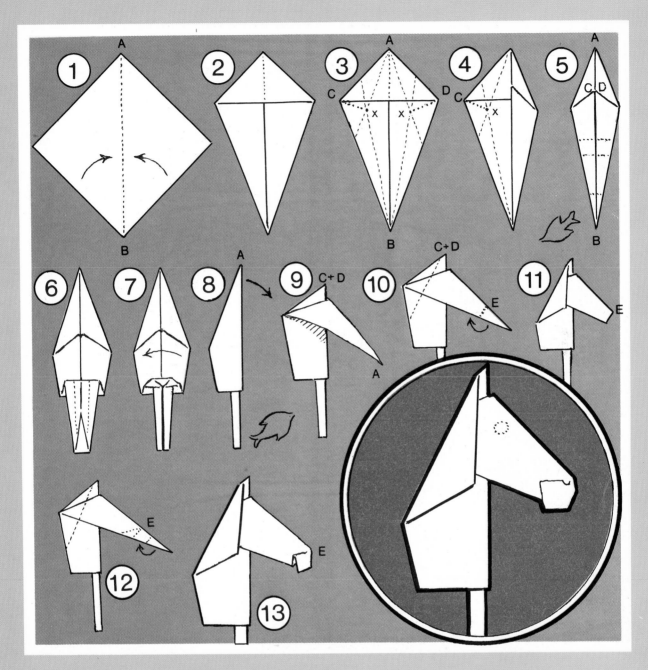

Going carefully, Rupert made this horse's head at the first attempt. (It was invented by a clever paperfolder, Martin Wall.) Take a square of thin paper. Fold it once as in Fig. 1, then fold both lower sides to the middle line (Fig. 2) and fold AC, BC, AD and BD in turn to the middle line to leave the pattern of creases in Fig. 3. Note the points marked X where the creases meet. Fold AD and BD together to the middle as far as you can and crease the line XD neatly (Fig. 4). Do the same with C (Fig. 5), making the points at C and D very sharp. To shorten the stem fold B up to A to form the top dotted line, bend B down again at the next line and fold the tip up to look like Fig. 6. Bend the lower sides inward by the new dotted lines and squash at the top to narrow the stem (Fig. 7). Fold the whole thing in half (Fig. 8). Pull A outward and turn it inside out (Fig. 9), revealing C and D which become the horse's ears. Decide on the length of head at E (Fig. 10) and reverse EA, pushing the tip under and out of sight. Bend down the left top corner for the mane and Fig. 11 is the simple horse's head. For a better nose return to Fig. 10, fold a smaller tip under and, using the two short dotted lines at E (Fig. 12), open the end and swivel it (Fig. 13) into the final position. If you mean to use it as a bookmark press it under something heavy. Draw the eyes rather high on the face.

RUPERT

"The gale has blown all these tiles down,"
Says Algy with a worried frown.

All night it has blown a fearful gale. Now Rupert goes out to see the damage. When he comes to Algy Pug's house he finds his chum glumly filling a barrow with tiles blown off his roof. When Algy says he must dump the tiles somewhere Rupert offers to push the wheelbarrow. Bingo, the clever pup, has the same problem—what to do with bits blown off his workshop. "Put them in Algy's wheelbarrow," says Rupert, "and we'll

and the GEMLINS

Poor Bingo, too, is in distress.
The gale has left his shed a mess.

"Dame Tansey's house is worst of all,"
Says Bingo. "We had better call."

look for a place to dump them." The pals decide that it will have to be outside the village and on their way out of Nutwood they come across Dame Tansey's cottage. It really has suffered in the gale and the chums find the poor old lady weeping. "Oh, dear," she wails. "Windows broken, shutters damaged, tiles blown off, fence knocked down. It will cost so much to mend I won't be able to buy coal for my stove."

Then he says, "I know how to do
Repairs to fence and shutters, too."

RUPERT AND HIS CHUMS HELP OUT

Young Algy's help is quite enough,
So Rupert goes to dump the stuff.

At length he finds the very spot
To dump the rubbish he has brought.

He tips the rubbish carefully
Into the hole left by the tree.

Then as he turns back, out it shoots
From somewhere underneath the roots.

"We must help the old lady in some way," Rupert whispers to the others. "I'm sure Algy and I could do some repairs," pipes up Bingo. "Rupert can find somewhere to dump all the broken stuff." The other two eagerly agree and Dame Tansey starts to brighten up at once. So while Algy and Bingo set about putting the house to rights Rupert sets off with the wheelbarrow. He hasn't gone far when he comes across a tree that has been blown down in the gale. "Whew!" he gasps. "What a hole it has left . . . hey, that's the very place to dump this rubbish!" He trundles the heavily laden barrow to the edge of the hole. Yes, it really is a big hole. Just the place. He tips the barrow and sends the broken tiles and splintered wood into the hole. He steps back rather pleased with himself and almost at once gives a yelp of alarm. For all his rubbish comes hurtling back out of the hole and he has to duck to avoid being hit by it. "What on earth's happening?" he cries.

RUPERT MEETS A GEMLIN

A man in miner's clothes peers out
And shouts, "Hey, watch what you're about!"

"Down there's our diamond mine, young bear.
How dare you dump your rubbish there!"

"Our diamond mine's deep underground.
Now you are here, I'll show you round."

The miner seals the entrance tight,
And Rupert feels a twinge of fright.

In the next instant there is a scrambling noise from the hole and a small, very angry face appears out of the darkness. It belongs to a little man who is wearing a miner's helmet with a lamp on it and holding a pickaxe. He tosses out the pickaxe and climbs after it. "How dare you throw your nasty rubbish down our diamond mine!" he shouts. "D-diamond mine?" exclaims Rupert. "I'd no idea there was a mine of any sort here. Oh dear, I am sorry!" The little man's frown fades: "I think you really are sorry." He pauses. "Didn't know there was a diamond mine here, eh?" he muses. "Well, now you're here would you like to see it?" "Oh please!" cries Rupert. "Right, then down you go," the little man laughs and ushers Rupert into the hole. Rupert finds that he is standing on a steep flight of steps cut into the earth. "Just a moment," says the man and while Rupert watches he blocks the entrance with a rock. This worries Rupert a bit.

RUPERT GOES UNDERGROUND

*At length they reach a sort of cage
To take them down to the next stage.*

*Into the lift and down they go
Towards the diamond mine below.*

*A truck stands on a railway line,
"Jump in! We'll soon be at the mine."*

*"I say," cries Rupert, "this is fun!"
As down the railway line they run.*

The little man sees that Rupert is worried. He smiles: "Don't be frightened. I just want to make sure no one else discovers the mine." He leads the way down and down until they come to a low tunnel that leads to a brightly lit chamber where a lift is waiting. They enter the lift, the man pulls a lever and slowly it begins to descend. Rupert's worries have quite gone now. "I say, this mine of yours must be awfully deep," he exclaims as the lift keeps going down. "Pretty deep," the little man chuckles. "But here we are." The lift stops and they get out and at once climb into something that looks like a tiny railway truck. Indeed, it is standing on narrow rails that disappear down a gentle slope. "This will take us down to where the real mining is done," the man explains. "Now hold tight." A brake is released and with a rumble the truck starts to move, gathering speed as it rattles downwards. "Oh, this is fun!" laughs Rupert.

RUPERT STARTS BACK BY BARGE

"We Gemlins mine a special gem,
Black diamonds—our King treasures them."

"Are those black diamonds?" Rupert blinks.
"Looks more like coal to me," he thinks.

Now to the palace it is borne,
And turned to gems that can be worn.

Rupert is told to leave by barge,
And finds himself alone in charge!

As the truck rumbles down the slope the little man explains, "I'm what's called a Gemlin. We're called that because we mine for gems, you know." Just then the truck comes to a stop in a well-lit gallery and Rupert sees lots of little men like his guide chipping at the rocky walls with pickaxes. The stuff they are mining is dumped on a moving belt. "I say, it looks just like coal!" Rupert bursts out. "Nothing of the kind!" retorts his guide. "The mine belongs to our king

and what we're mining here are black diamonds." The little man leads the way beside the moving belt until they come to an underground river where barges are being loaded with the black lumps. "They're on the way to the palace to be made into gems," he explains. "Well, thank you," Rupert says. "Now I'd better get back. My pals will wonder what's happened to me." "Then step aboard," smiles the Gemlin and ushers Rupert on to an empty barge nearby.

RUPERT LOSES CONTROL

"You'll reach two tunnels. You must take
The left-hand one. Make no mistake."

Now Rupert poles his way along
Helped by the current, fast and strong.

"Those are the tunnels," he decides.
Towards the left the barge he guides.

But though he tries with all his might,
The current pulls him to the right.

"B-but how do I get back on a barge?" Rupert wants to know. "Simple," says the Gemlin. "Use this barge pole to punt your way downstream." He smiles when he sees that Rupert is uncertain. "It really is quite easy," he says. "You'll soon get used to it. Just remember that when you come to two tunnels that you must take the left-hand one. You'll find a path beside it that will take you back to near where we met." And so Rupert pushes off and although at first he is rather nervous he soon finds that he is getting used to poling the heavy barge along. At last, ahead of him, he sees the two tunnels. There is daylight at the end of the left-hand one he has been told to take. The other, which has a crown above it, leads into darkness. "Whew! I must admit I'm rather glad to see daylight again," Rupert thinks and he pushes hard to steer the barge to the left. But nothing happens. The stream is flowing much faster and he cannot control the barge.

RUPERT GOES THE WRONG WAY

"I must go left at any cost!"
And then, oh, dear! His pole is lost!

There's nothing he can do to shift
The vessel from its headlong drift.

Upon a jetty three guards stand.
"Help!" Rupert cries. "Please help me land!"

"Quick! Get ashore!" one Gemlin snaps.
"Then you'll explain yourself perhaps!"

"Oh my! This is awful!" Rupert gasps as he pushes harder and harder against the pole. Then just when he thinks he is getting the barge to go to the left a swirl of water catches it. The heavy vessel swings sideways and in trying to keep his balance Rupert lets go of the pole. He grabs at it in vain for it is already out of reach. Now he is thoroughly scared. He crouches on the stern of the barge and watches the dark right-hand tunnel getting nearer and nearer. Next moment he is enveloped in darkness with only the swish of the water to tell him he is still moving along. Then he gives a great sigh of relief for ahead he can see a gleam of light that gets bigger and brighter until the barge sweeps out into a cavern that is brightly lit. Just inside it is a jetty and on it is standing a group of little men. Rupert doesn't have to shout for help for as the barge nears the jetty the little men catch it with spear-like boathooks and pull it in.

RUPERT MEETS THE GEMLIN KING

"You must have come down here to spy!
You'll pay for this!" the Gemlins cry.

On Rupert now the guards take hold
And cry, "Our ruler must be told!"

Sternly the King says he must know
What Rupert's doing here below.

But when he's heard the story through,
He says, "I do believe that's true."

The faces Rupert finds himself looking into are anything but friendly. He is dragged out of the boat by two of the little men. Before he can even begin to explain, the third of his captors shouts, "Spy! You have come to spy on us. Oh, the king shall hear of this!" And Rupert finds himself bundled up steps which lead to a narrow path skirting a cavern. He tries to explain about losing the barge pole but is told to be quiet. At last he notices that the light is brighter and he feels carpet under his feet. He looks up. And there, ahead of him, perched on a throne is the King of the Gemlins. He listens to the guards but unlike them he also listens to Rupert, and when the little bear finishes his tale, rises and gazes at him. "You look honest," he says at last. "Perhaps you did drift here by mistake. But now you are here and I must decide what is to be done with you." "Oh, please," Rupert starts to say. "Quiet!" shouts a guard.

RUPERT IS OFFERED A GIFT

"Come, little bear!" Then Rupert's led
Into a room that lies ahead.

"You cannot work down here, it's clear.
You're far too tall for us, I fear."

"Black diamonds are made into things
Of beauty—bracelets, brooches, rings."

The treasure chest is opened. "Pray,
Choose what you'd like to take away."

Rupert's knees are shaking as the Gemlin King stands deep in thought. Then the little monarch steps down from his throne and beckons to Rupert to follow him. He leads the way to a low archway of jagged rock and strides through, then turns and watches Rupert. "H'm, I thought so," murmurs the King as Rupert has to stoop to follow. "Had you been small enough to walk straight through you could have stayed and joined my Gemlins. But you're too big." "Thank goodness," thinks Rupert.

"Pity," says the King. "I'm sure we'd have got on well. Now, follow me!" And a very puzzled Rupert hurries after him and finds himself at last in another cavern where Gemlins are making jewellery from the black diamonds. "This is where we store our black diamond treasure," the King says. At his command a huge treasure chest is opened. It is full of brooches, necklaces and rings. "Now, little bear!" cries the King. "You may choose a gift to take home with you!"

55

RUPERT MAKES A CHOICE

He thinks of Poor Dame Tansey's plight
And asks, "Plain lumps, please, if I might."

"The storekeeper!" a guard is bid,
And bangs his spear upon a lid.

"Now storeman, hark to what I say.
Some plain black lumps to take away."

A length of rope is handed out.
"Now pull!" The storeman gives a shout.

Rupert lifts a sparkling black necklace from the treasure chest and is admiring it when he suddenly remembers what Dame Tansey said about not having enough money left to buy coal. "Oh, please, your Majesty," he says, "would it be possible for me to have instead some ordinary lumps of coal—er, I mean black diamonds—for a friend of mine?" "You know, I have heard it called coal before," says the King. "But only we Gemlins can make black diamonds from it. But if that's what you want ..." He leads the way to where lids are set into the floor and tells a guard, "Summon the storekeeper!" The man taps on one of the lids and up pops a grimy face. "Ho, storekeeper!" commands the King. "Prepare some black diamond chunks for this little bear to take away." "At once, sire," says the man and he pulls out a rope which he hands to Rupert. "Just hold on to that for a moment, young sir," he asks and pops back into the hole.

RUPERT SAYS GOODBYE

On Rupert's rope a sack is tied.
He feels the heavy lumps inside.

"Upon my word, I do declare,"
The King says, "you're a thoughtful bear!"

"Oh," Rupert cries, "I thought you would
Know, as a bargeman, I'm no good!"

"A bargeman will escort you back.
Just hand aboard your heavy sack."

Rupert wonders what is happening down below as he stands holding the rope. At length he feels a tug on it and the storekeeper calls, "You can pull it up now, young sir." On the end of the rope is a small, but surprisingly heavy, sack. "It must be a sack of coal!" Rupert exclaims. Then he remembers and corrects himself: "Of course, I mean black diamonds. Oh, and how pleased Dame Tansey will be with it!" "You're a thoughtful little bear to help a friend so," the King says as he leads the way back through the tunnels. At last they come out on the landing stage where Rupert arrived. But what a difference. This time the guards stand respectfully to attention. When he sees an empty barge waiting for him Rupert is dismayed. "Your Majesty, as you know, I'm not much good at managing barges." The King smiles. "Don't worry," he says. "This time one of my best boatman will go with you." And so Rupert hands his sack to the boatman and climbs aboard.

RUPERT SETS OFF ALONE

"Farewell!" As Rupert's visit ends,
He's sad to leave his new-found friends.

The other tunnel isn't far.
"Right!" says the bargeman. "Here we are!"

"Now you must walk, if you don't mind,
And climb the flight of steps you'll find."

As Rupert sets off on his own,
He wishes he were not alone.

The kindly little King is sad to see Rupert go, and as the barge moves off he calls, "Farewell, little bear! I wish you could have stayed!" And Rupert, who feels quite glum himself, almost wishes that he could, and cries, "Thank you, your Majesty, and goodbye!" The return journey is upstream and as Rupert watches the Gemlin boatman having to use all his strength to push the barge against the current he realises he could never have made the journey on his own. At last, though, the barge reaches the entrance to the tunnel Rupert should have taken earlier. Skilfully the Gemlin steers the craft into it and moors beside a very narrow path. "This is where you get out, young sir," he tells Rupert. "I have to turn back now." Feeling just a bit uneasy, Rupert puts his sack ashore and scrambles after it. "What do I do now?" he wants to know. "Oh, it's easy," replies the Gemlin. "Just follow this path until you come to some steps." So off Rupert sets again.

RUPERT GETS OUT OF THE MINE

At last he finds a long, steep flight
Of steps which rise towards the light.

He spies the fallen tree below:
"That's good! Now my way home, I know."

The little bear climbs down the hill,
And groans, "Here's all that rubbish still!"

The entrance is so well concealed,
Its secret will not be revealed.

Rupert now begins to realise just how heavy the little sack of coal really is as he trudges along the waterside path. It is much longer than he expected and after a while he wonders if somehow he has missed the steps he has been told to look out for. Then suddenly there they are and Rupert heaves a sigh of relief. But the hardest part of his return journey lies ahead for now he has to climb as far as he came down in the lift. But just when he is about to give up he sees daylight ahead and in a moment is out in the open looking down on the fallen tree where his adventure began. He is relieved to see that Algy's wheelbarrow is safe and he scrambles down to it. Of course, he realises with dismay, the rubbish is still there too. "Oh well," he tells himself, "I shall just have to load it back into the barrow and find some other place to dump it." Then he peers into the hole under the tree. The mine entrance is so well sealed no one would guess it was there.

RUPERT IS HELPED

"Oh dear," sighs Rupert. "This is grim."
Just then a car stops close to him.

"It's the Professor's servant. Hi!
What luck that you should just chance by!"

The little servant lends a hand.
"Oh thanks!" says Rupert. "This is grand."

"We'll tip the rubbish in my car.
I'll dump it later. There we are!"

Exhausted after his long climb back to the surface, Rupert stands gazing at the rubbish which is scattered all around. "It makes me even more tired just looking at it," he mutters. "But I suppose I better get it into the barrow and find some other place to dump it." Just then a car horn sounds and Rupert turns to see the little servant of his friend the old Professor. "Hello, young Rupert," calls the little man. "You look pretty glum. What's wrong, eh? Lost your way?" Then he spies all the rubbish. "I say, you didn't scatter this mess, did you?" "Of course not," Rupert says and starts to explain how it comes to be there. This leads him into telling about his adventure and as he talks the little man helps him to gather up the rubbish and dump it in the back of his little truck. "I'll get rid of it for you later," he promises. "I'll find a place where it won't bother people. Now would you like a lift?" "Very much, thanks," Rupert says.

RUPERT ASKS THE PROFESSOR

The servant hears his story through,
Then begs, "Please tell my master, too."

"Please," Rupert asks the kind old man,
"Tell me what this is if you can."

"Give me a lump, it would be best
To put it through a special test."

"This super kind of coal will blaze
For many months," the old man says.

As they bowl along the country lanes on the way to Nutwood, the little servant gets Rupert to tell him again about the black diamonds and how the Gemlins were able to make it into jewellery. "Amazing, amazing," the servant repeats. "Do you know, I'm sure my master would like to hear about this and maybe have a look at the black diamonds you've brought back." "Why, of course," Rupert says. And in a little while the old Professor is greeting his young friend warmly and inviting him into his castle home. They go straight to the Professor's workroom and Rupert does not spend time telling his story again but simply hands the Professor a piece of black diamond from his sack. "Can you tell me what this really is?" he asks. The old man examines it very closely then exclaims, "It *is* coal, but a sort I've never seen before. We must test it!" He heats a bit of it in a small furnace then puts it in a sort of cauldron. "Remarkable!" he gasps.

RUPERT IS BACK WITH HIS PALS

"A very small amount will last
Until the winter is well past!"

"Dame Tansey will be pleased, it's plain."
Thinks Rupert, setting off again.

"Oh good!" exclaims the little bear.
"Algy and Bingo are still there."

Says Rupert, "I've been busy too.
I've something strange to show to you!"

"What's remarkable about it?" Rupert wants to know. "Don't you see?" the Professor cries. "It keeps glowing brightly and leaves absolutely no ash. It's quite amazing stuff. Never seen any coal like it. It's quite clear it will go on burning for months. May I keep this piece?" "Of course you may," Rupert agrees. "There's plenty left for Dame Tansey. And since it lasts so long it will save her lots of money." Then he loads the sack into Algy's wheelbarrow and sets off for Dame Tansey's cottage. From some way off he sees that his two pals are still working around the cottage. "Hello, Rupert!" Bingo greets him. "Where have you been? It's taken you ages. In fact, we've almost finished the repairs, haven't we, Algy." "Indeed we have, you old slacker," Algy laughs. "Not at all," Rupert says. "Just you wait till you hear my story and see what I've brought for Dame Tansey!" "Come on then, let's see it!" Bingo cries.

RUPERT AND HIS PALS GO HOME

The three decide to lay a fire,
Just sticks and paper they require.

Dame Tansey can't believe her eyes.
"A bucketful of coal!" she cries.

The poor old lady's thrilled to learn,
For months and months her fire will burn.

Of all her worries she's quite free,
Thanks to the thoughtful Nutwood three.

Algy and Bingo can't believe their ears when Rupert tells them what the old Professor has said about the black diamonds. "Come on, let's try it then," says Bingo who always likes to know how things work. And so while Rupert tips the black diamonds into a bucket his pals collect paper and sticks to make a fire. They are ready to fill the grate when Dame Tansey returns. "A bucketful of coal!" she marvels. "Why, I haven't been able to afford coal for weeks." "But this is a very special sort of coal," laughs Rupert and asks her to light the fire. In a very short while the fire is crackling away merrily and Dame Tansey sits wide-eyed and smiling at Rupert's promise that the coal will last for months. "Oh, my!" laughs the old lady. "You've all been so good, repairing my house and giving me this wonderful coal, thank you, thank you!" Later as the friends leave Dame Tansey's house Bingo says, "Come on now, Rupert, you're going to tell us the whole adventure!"

The two foxes play a trick on Rupert that leads to a strange journey for the little bear and a change in the weather.

RUPERT WANTS TO TOBOGGAN

Says Rupert, "Since there is no snow,
On frosty ground I'll have a go."

As he takes his toboggan out,
He hears Bill Badger give a shout.

For days the weather in Nutwood has been bitterly cold. But the snow Rupert keeps hoping for does not appear. "Oh dear, this is so tiresome," he sighs. "I so want to have a go on my toboggan." Then he has an idea. He finds his Daddy who is working in the garden and says, "There's quite a lot of very slippery frost about and I wondered if I might be able to use my toboggan on it. Do you think it might work?" Mr. Bear looks doubtful: "I don't think so." Then seeing that Rupert is very keen to go tobogganing, he adds, "Still, it might be worth trying." So off scampers the little bear to find a good place to try out his idea. But he has not gone far when someone calls, "Hey, Rupert, where are you off to with that toboggan?" He turns to see his pal Bill Badger running towards him.

the SNOW PUZZLE

RUPERT MEETS THE SQUIRE

*"Of course, use my estate, but, please,
Keep a lookout for my lost keys."*

*Says Rupert, "We must watch that hump,
Or we could have a nasty bump."*

When Bill hears of Rupert's idea to toboggan on frost he says, "Mmm, it might just work. But we'll need a long downhill run to keep moving. Let's find the right sort of slope." The two pals have reached the outskirts of Nutwood when they meet the Squire. When the old gentleman hears what they plan to do he smiles and says, "Well, there are plenty of good long slopes on my estate. You're welcome to try them if you like." He ushers the delighted pair through his gates. "You can try tobogganing here to your hearts' content," he tells them. Then as he turns to go he adds, "By the way, keep your eyes open for a bunch of my keys I dropped yesterday." The pals promise to keep a lookout. As they start uphill they see a strange hump in the grass. "Let's keep clear of that," says Rupert. "It could cause a nasty spill."

RUPERT'S CHUM TAKES A TUMBLE

They reach the top and start at last,
When something white goes flashing past.

"A snowball, Bill!" "I say, that's queer,"
Says Bill. "For no snow's fallen here!"

"Hold tight!" And Rupert pushes Bill,
Who hurtles on his way downhill.

The ride without snow's just too rough,
And Bill can't hang on tight enough.

At the top Rupert and Bill find a promising slope. Bill volunteers to go first and Rupert is about to give him a push when something white flashes past their heads. "Hey, who threw that?" yells Bill angrily and jumps off the toboggan. He is starting towards some bushes when a shout from Rupert stops him. "I say, Bill, this stuff's snow!" "Impossible!" exclaims Bill. "We've had no snow." Then he examines the white stuff Rupert has scooped up. "You're right!" he says. "But how ... ?" The pals puzzle over the snow and who could have thrown it. But no more appears and since there is no sign of anyone they decide to go on with the tobogganing. Rupert gives a hefty push. The toboggan races off, swaying and bumping alarmingly. Bill struggles to control it, but suddenly it hits a bump, flies into the air, overturns and poor Bill is pitched headfirst over some bushes.

RUPERT IS SNOWBALLED AGAIN

"Careful!" cries Jill Frost with a frown.
"You very nearly knocked me down!"

"No snow for Nutwood this year, no!
The Weather Clerk's arranged it so."

"I think I should go home," says Bill.
"I ache all over since that spill."

"Here come more snowballs!" Rupert cries.
Jill Frost just can't believe her eyes.

As Rupert plunges into the bushes after Bill he hears a shrill voice scolding, "Do be careful! You nearly knocked me over!" Next moment he sees his pal lying on the ground looking up at a strangely clad little person. "Why, Jack Frost!" he starts to say then he sees the newcomer is a girl. "Do you know my brother Jack?" she demands. Rupert explains that he has met Jack several times and asks how he is. "Busy elsewhere," says the girl.

"That's why I'm here doing his Nutwood job. I'm Jill Frost." "Oh, I say, are we going to have snow after all?" asks Rupert. "I'm afraid not," says Jill. "The Clerk of the Weather hasn't arranged for any for Nutwood." Just then Bill says, "I do ache after that spill. I'd best go home, I think. You stay here with Jill." And off he limps. He has hardly gone when another volley of snowballs narrowly misses Rupert and Jill.

RUPERT HEARS THE SNOW IS OLD

"Who threw those?" cries the little bear.
"I'm sure they came from over there!"

Rupert is just in time to see
The foxes dash off in high glee.

"This snow," says Jill, "is one year old!
The Weather Clerk just must be told."

"I'll take you with me, little bear."
Jill throws some powder in the air.

"Right, this time I'm going to find out who threw those snowballs!" vows Rupert and runs towards a copse from where he is sure the snowballs came. Pushing through the bushes he is just in time to see the Fox brothers, Freddy and Ferdy, dash off giggling, their arms full of snowballs. He turns back to Jill to tell her. "But where did they get snow?" he adds. "That's the mystery." "More of a mystery than you think," retorts Jill who has picked up a handful. "This is *last year's* snow! I can tell. The Clerk of the Weather must be told. There's something very odd here." She thinks for a moment. "Rupert," she says, "I want you to come, too. You see, I've played so many pranks on the Clerk he mightn't believe me. He'll believe you, though." "But how ... ? Rupert begins. "Simple!" Jill laughs. "Lie on the toboggan. Hold tight. Right?" And she throws some powder into the air.

RUPERT RIDES THE FROSTBOW

*Says Jill, "I've summoned up a gale
To take us straight there without fail."*

*They're swept up high and travel by
A frozen rainbow in the sky.*

*And as they reach the frostbow's top,
Jill warns, "Don't let that snowball drop!"*

*"The Weather Clerk lives down there, and
In just a moment we shall land."*

"That powder is to summon a wind to take us," Jill explains. "Hark, can you hear it coming?" Rupert listens and in the distance he can hear a howling growing ever louder. Suddenly the noise is all around him and Rupert finds himself swept high into the air, still clutching his snowball. He feels much less frightened when he sees Jill flying along beside him. Now they are travelling along a sparkling band in the sky. "It's a frozen rainbow!" shouts Jill. "A frostbow!" At the top of the frostbow Jill calls, "We shall be going down now, even faster. So hold on and don't drop that snowball!" Down, down they race, faster and faster until Rupert thinks they will never be able to stop. Then through a bank of cloud they shoot and just ahead lies a cluster of strange spires and towers. "We're here!" Jill cries. "This is where the Clerk of the Weather lives!"

RUPERT MEETS THE WEATHER MAN

Once they are down Jill leads the way
To where the Weather Clerk holds sway.

Jill's played tricks on the Clerk before,
And now he thinks she's up to more.

"Oh, please, Jill's sure that this snowball
Is truly part of last year's fall."

"Yes, this is last year's snow, all right.
By now it should have melted quite!"

Jill seems to have some strange control over the wind for at a clap of her hands it changes to a gentle breeze which wafts them both down on to a sort of terrace. Jill knows the way and, telling Rupert to leave behind his toboggan, she leads the way up a flight of stairs. It leads to a tower where the Clerk himself is working. The fussy little man's face falls when he sees Jill. "Oh, dear, not more of your tricks," he sighs. "Oh, no," says Jill. "This is truly important. This little bear, Rupert, will tell you about it." So rather nervously Rupert launches into his story of the mysterious snowballs and how Jill said that they were last year's snow. "Oh, my!" exclaims the little man. "I suspect she is playing tricks on you, too." He agrees, however, to examine the snow, and when he does he can't believe his eyes. "It is last year's snow!" he cries. "But how has it lasted?"

RUPERT IS PROMISED SNOW

"I keep a jar of each year's snow,
But last year I forgot, you know."

"And so I'm glad of this snowball.
Now I have samples of them all."

"You do want snow? I think I can
Do that for you!" exclaims the man.

"A blizzard Nutwood's way I'll send;
As much snow as you want, young friend."

Shaking his head, the Clerk of the Weather leads the friends to a set of shelves stacked with jars. Each jar has a year marked on it. "Snow," explains the Clerk. "I have a sample of every year's snow right back to the year 1820. Every year, that is, except last year's. Strangely enough, I forgot to take a sample in time. So I'm very grateful for this lot you've brought. Now my records will be up to date." "Rupert is very disappointed there's to be no snow in Nutwood this year," Jill breaks in. "Disappointed?" says the Clerk. "You mean you *want* heavy snow?" "Oh, please!" cries Rupert. "H'm," murmurs the Clerk. "I may just be in time ..." He consults a ticker tape then leads the way to a strange wheel thing where he pulls levers and presses buttons. "There!" he says at last. "I have switched a blizzard meant for Alaska to your Nutwood. Now, quick to the launching pad!"

RUPERT AND JILL FLY BACK

"Here comes the blizzard," Jill declares,
And for their flight home she prepares.

They're both swept up and off they go,
So swift and high amid the snow.

Now Rupert's on his homeward flight,
And darkness soon gives way to light.

Then home at last and down they sweep
To land in snow so soft and deep.

Wondering what on earth is going to happen now, Rupert is hustled by Jill out of the Clerk of the Weather's workshop then through passages and up stairs, collecting Rupert's toboggan on the way. At last they reach a high platform. "We're not a moment too soon," Jill pants. "Look!" And Rupert turns to see a huge bank of dark cloud looming over them. Before the little bear realises what is happening he is swept off his feet by a howling snow storm and carried into the air, clutching his toboggan. "Don't struggle!" cries Jill. "Just let the storm carry you along." When he does relax Rupert finds that he is really quite comfortable. But he still finds the darkness and the howling of the wind rather frightening and he is glad when it starts to grow light and he finds they are gradually dropping to earth. He gets ready for a bump but instead lands gently in deep, soft snow.

RUPERT HELPS IN A RESCUE

"Please thank the Weather Clerk for me,"
Smiles Rupert, happy as can be.

The Squire's gamekeeper tries to shift
Snow from a mound deep in a drift.

"There's someone trapped here, I'm afraid!
Lend me a hand. Here, take this spade!"

They reach a door into the mound.
In it a bunch of keys is found.

"Is this better?" laughs Jill as Rupert picks himself up. "Oh, yes!" he says. "I do hope everyone else thinks so." "They'll like it a lot more than what they were going to get," Jill says. "Frost, fog and icy winds!" Then she turns and skips away, crying, "Well, I must get on with my work!" "Thank the Clerk of the Weather for being so kind!" Rupert calls after her. Later as he makes his way homeward through the Squire's estate he sees the gamekeper clearing snow from a mound. "Hello, Mr. Foster," Rupert says when he gets up to him. "What are you doing?" The man holds up his hand. "Listen! Can you hear voices from inside this mound?" he asks. Rupert listens hard. "Yes!" he exclaims. "Then help me dig them out!" the man cries and hands him a spade. They dig desperately and in a little while they uncover a wheelbarrow, then a low door with a bunch of keys still in it.

RUPERT SEES THE HIDDEN SNOW

"There is a sort of vault inside,"
The man says as the door swings wide.

Frozen and scared, the foxes know
They've had a narrow squeak below.

"It's full of snow, heaped on the floor!
And even on that bench there's more."

"We went for more snow for a game,
And then that awful blizzard came."

"I thought this was just a great heap of snow," Rupert exclaims. "No," the gamekeeper says as he tugs to open the door, "it's a sort of vault below a grassy mound." "Of course," Rupert thinks, "that's the bump Bill and I saw on our way up the hill." The heavy door now swings open to reveal Freddy and Ferdy Fox shaking with cold. "Br-r-r!" Ferdy shivers as they stagger out on stiff legs. "W-w-we're f-f-frozen!" Curious to see inside the strange underground room, Rupert ventures into it. In it he sees snow heaped on the floor and on low benches too. "What's snow doing inside?" he wonders. "And why were the foxes in here?" He returns to the others in time to hear Ferdy say, "It was awful in there. We went in to get some more snow, then that blizzard came and snowed up the door." "Oh yes," Freddy wails. "It all happened so quickly we didn't have a chance to get out. And it was so dark and cold!"

RUPERT HEARS THE FOXES' TALE

*"One of the bunch of keys we found
Fitted the door into this mound."*

*"We found the snow stored in there, so
We took some just for fun, you know."*

*"That was last year's snow, little bear;
The Squire stored quite a lot in there."*

*The man says, "You shall make amends,
And clear the Squire's drive, my friends!"*

Now he is sure the foxes are not really hurt the gamekeeper holds up the bunch of keys he has taken from the door. "The Squire lost these keys yesterday," he says grimly. "And I think you two have some explaining to do." So Ferdy and Freddy tell their story. They found the keys, they say, when they were taking a shortcut through the estate. They discovered that the keys fitted the door into the mound and when they found the snow inside they took some for fun. But when they are finished Rupert still has some questions. "Mr. Foster," he begins, "Jill Frost says the snow in there is last year's snow." "True," chuckles the gamekeeper. "Been there since last winter, but that is something for the Squire to tell you about. Meanwhile these foxes are going to make amends for their pranks." Ordering the brothers to bring the wheelbarrow, he leads them off to clear the snow from the Squire's drive.

RUPERT TELLS BILL HIS STORY

As Rupert's sled speeds down the hill,
He thinks, "I know—I'll call on Bill."

Now Rupert tells his story through,
Of last year's snow and this year's too.

At home he finds the Squire is there,
Deep in a talk with Mr. Bear.

"I'm glad to have my keys once more.
Now I'll explain about my store."

As he races downhill on his way home, Rupert decides to call on Bill to see how he is after his spill. Mrs. Badger is clearing snow from the path when he arrives and ushers him indoors where Bill is snug in an armchair. Once Rupert is sure Bill is feeling much better and they've laid plans for tobogganing next day, he tells his chum about his adventure. "I still don't know, though, why last year's snow was stored in that underground place," he winds up. "I

shall have to ask the Squire." And strangely enough, who should be talking to Mr. Bear when Rupert gets home but the Squire himself. "Ah, the Squire has something to say to you, Rupert," says Mr. Bear. "I've just been talking to my gamekeeper," the Squire begins, "and he tells me you helped him rescue the foxes and, as it happens, find my keys. Thank you! Mr. Foster also told me you wondered why I'd kept last year's snow. Well, I'll tell you."

76

RUPERT LEARNS THE SECRET

*"Here is the plan in which I found
An old ice-house beneath that mound."*

*"I tried it out with snow, you see.
It kept it fresh indefinitely."*

*And now the foxes come along
To say they're sorry they've done wrong.*

*All is forgiven. "You shall share
Tomorrow's fun!" laughs Rupert Bear.*

The Squire unrolls an old paper he is holding and lays it on the table. "Last year," he says, "I found this old plan of all the buildings in my grounds. In it I discovered that the cellar under that mound was an old ice-house. Snow and ice could be stored in it all year round so that the owner of the estate could keep things cool in warm weather. I tried it out with some of last year's snow and you've seen how fresh it still is." So at last Rupert knows the answer to the snow puzzle. As the Squire and he walk to the gate Rupert says, "It was lucky you kept some of last year's snow." But before he can explain about the Clerk of the Weather, the two foxes appear and mumble their apologies to the Squire. "And we're sorry for throwing snowballs at you, Rupert," Ferdy says. "Oh, that doesn't matter," laughs the little bear. "You missed, anyway! I say, why not come tobogganing with us tomorrow?"

RUPERT

The snowball battle is great fun,
At least, till Edward Trunk throws one.

The great Nutwood snowball fight is in full swing. Rupert and Willie Mouse are giving as good as they get from Algy Pug, Bill Badger and Edward Trunk. Then Edward, who can throw hard but not straight, aims one at Willie, misses and hits Rupert right in the eye. It hurts and poor Edward is terribly upset, but luckily old Sailor Sam happens to be passing and sees what has occurred.

and the RED BOX

It hits poor Rupert in the eye
Just as old Sailor Sam comes by.

Sam has some lotion in his shack
And soon puts right that nasty smack.

"Come on, I've just the thing for that eye," says Sam and leads Rupert into his shack where he produces a bottle of lotion. He bathes the little bear's eye with it and in no time the pain has quite gone. Rupert wonders what he can do to show his gratitude. "I know," he says, "I'll tidy up your ship models and all your charts." "Thank you very much," smiles Sam. "But I like 'em as they are."

When Rupert wants his thanks to show,
Sam says, "That's kind of you, but no."

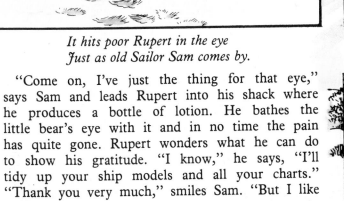

RUPERT TAKES A TUMBLE

So Rupert and his pals decide
That on the frozen stream they'll slide.

But Rupert stumbles, Bill trips—Smack!
Next Willie—and the ice goes "Crack!"

Podgy comes skating up the stream;
"Stop! Broken ice!" the others scream.

Oh, too late Podgy understands!
Skids, falls and on the ice he lands.

So off Rupert goes back to his friends who have decided that after the accident with Edward's snowball they should find something else to do. "I've got it!" Rupert cries. "The stream's frozen over. Let's make a slide on it!" Everyone is in favour and so down to the stream they troop and are soon whooping with delight as they slither and slide on the ice. But accidents are not over for the day. Rupert takes a sudden tumble and the others who are close behind pile on top of him. They pick themselves up laughing, then they see that their fall has cracked the ice. They gather on the bank and are discussing what to do next when suddenly, skating up the stream comes Podgy Pig—straight for the crack. "Look out, Podgy! Stop! Broken ice!" the pals yell. But at first the plump skater doesn't seem to understand. And when he does it is too late. Desperately he tries to stop. But in vain.

RUPERT FINDS THE RED BOX

"Help! Help! I'm sinking!" Podgy bawls
As through the broken ice he falls.

Rupert and Bill each grab a hand
And pull poor Podgy to dry land.

Cross and shivering, Podgy waits
While wire's untangled from his skates.

The wire has Rupert mystified;
A red box to its end is tied.

With a great crack the broken ice gives way. And with an even greater yelp of dismay Podgy falls into the water. The pals dash to the spot where Podgy is floundering and gasping. Bill and Rupert grab a hand each and with help from the others pull Podgy ashore. "Oh, d-d-dear, I'm s-s-soaked!" he wails. "I m-m-must g-g-get home at once!" But when he tries to rise he finds something tangled round his skates. "It looks like wire," says Willie. "Wait a moment

while I untangle it." As Willie frees the skates and Podgy shivers and wails Rupert is wondering about the wire. He is still holding it and when he gives it a slight tug he feels something move under the water. He is so very curious that he stays behind when the others go off with Podgy. Making sure he has a good foothold on the bank, he starts pulling in the wire, yards and yards of it. Then at last an old red box breaks the surface of the stream.

RUPERT ASKS FOR HELP

So off to Podgy's house he goes,
And to his chum the strange box shows.

"There's no sign of a keyhole there,"
The locksmith says, "but don't despair."

"Run, ask that scientific man!
If anyone can help, he can!"

"You can't find a way in, you say?
Let's look at it through this X-ray."

Rupert feels that Podgy should have the box so he takes it to the little pig's house where he finds him sitting up in bed. "I must say it's a pretty dull sort of thing," Podgy says ungraciously when Rupert shows him the box. He shakes it: "Doesn't seem to be anything in it. And even if there were you wouldn't be able to get at it since there doesn't seem to be a lid or a keyhole. Here, you can have it." Rupert is still very curious about the box and he takes it to a locksmith. "Sorry," says the man, "but without a keyhole I can't help you ... but wait!" He takes Rupert to the door and points to an old man in the street. "Now, he's a very clever scientist. I'm sure if anyone can help he can." Rupert dashes after the old man. A few minutes later, having told the scientist his problem, Rupert is staring at a strange machine in the man's workroom. "Let's take a look through this X-ray," the man says.

RUPERT OPENS THE BOX

The old man says, "How very quaint.
The keyhole's covered up with paint."

So Rupert perches on a stool
And probes the keyhole with a tool.

At first the contents of the box
Seem dull, when it at last unlocks.

He realises with a start
That this could be a treasure chart.

Rupert gazes wide-eyed while the scientist puts the red box on a special stand and looks at it through a sort of camera. "H'm," he says at last. "Keyhole and lid have been covered over with paint, that's all. Here, I'll give you a sharp tool to pick it off." He peers over Rupert's shoulder while the little bear picks and pokes at the thick red paint. At last lid and keyhole are revealed. The scientist sorts through a drawerful of old keys till he finds one to fit. "Right," he says. "Your box, so you open it!" Holding his breath, Rupert turns the key and prises up the lid and ... how disappointing! All that is inside is a folded paper. "Well, don't just stand there," says the man. "Open it up!" Carefully Rupert unfolds the stiff old paper. "Why, it's a map, a chart of an island!" he exclaims. "Now why should anyone want to hide it in a box? ... Oh! Unless it was a treasure map!"

RUPERT SHOWS SAM THE MAP

The man says, "Oh, I'm much too old
To go and search for buried gold."

"Of course," thinks Rupert, "Sam's the one
To know the best thing to be done."

"A pirate island, little bear!
There could be treasure buried there."

"I'll search for it, that's what I'll do,"
Cries Sam. "And, Rupert, you'll come too!"

"What a pity I'm too old to go searching for treasure," says the scientist. "I'd liked to have found out if that really is a treasure chart." At the mention of "chart" Rupert knows the very person to ask about the map. Sailor Sam, of course. His shack is full of charts. So thanking the scientist, Rupert hurries off to Sam's and just as he gets near the shack he sees the old sailor ahead of him. The moment Sam sets eyes on the chart he is excited. "Aye,

this here's a pirate island, beyond doubt!" he cries. "Oh, and there may well be treasure hidden there! We mustn't waste a moment! You ask your Mummy if you can sail with me and we'll go this very night!" "Oh, I'm sure Mummy will say I may go," Rupert laughs. "She knows I'll be safe with you." "Right," says Sam, "we'll meet outside your garden at dusk." And as Rupert makes off Sam calls, "And if you can find a pal to help with the search so much the better!"

RUPERT AND HIS PALS SET OFF

Then Willie Mouse is told the tale
And vows that with his chum he'll sail.

At dusk when it is time to start,
Sam brings provisions in a cart.

All through the night Sam pushes on.
He says, "We'll reach the coast at dawn."

And, sure enough, at break of day,
They find Sam's cutter in the bay.

As he runs home Rupert meets Willie Mouse. "Why," he thinks, "Willie would be the very one to come with us." And sure enough as soon as he has told his chum about the map and before he has had a chance to say anything about going with Sailor Sam, Willie cries, "Oh, let's go and search for it, Rupert, please!" And so at dusk, with both their Mummies' permission, the chums are waiting for Sam. When he does appear he is pushing a barrow loaded with provisions.

"Climb aboard, mates!" laughs Sam. "And better make yourselves comfortable for we have a long trip before we reach the coast." "How long will it be?" the chums want to know. "Take us till dawn," the old sailor replies. "So settle down and get a bit of rest if you can." All through the night Sam trundles the barrow and sure enough as daylight breaks they reach the coast and there, nestling in a rocky bay, is Sailor Sam's trim little cutter.

RUPERT SPIES THE ISLAND

When all their things are stowed at last,
They hoist their sail and off they cast.

A gentle breeze begins to blow,
And out to sea the three friends go.

Rupert and Willie think it's grand,
Even although they're far from land.

A broad lagoon before them lies.
"This is our island!" Rupert cries.

Rupert and Willie love Sam's boat from the moment they set eyes on it with its shining woodwork, taut rigging and neatly furled sail. Eagerly they join in unloading the provisions from the wheelbarrow and transferring them to the boat's lockers; food, drink, extra rope—"Never know when it'll come in useful," Sam says—and waterproof clothing just in case they meet any storms. Then as the sun comes up over the horizon they set sail and put to sea.

Sam consults the chart from the red box and turns the boat's bow towards where the island should lie. A steady gentle breeze springs up to fill the cutter's sails and the trim little craft fairly skims over the waves. Rupert and Willie volunteer to keep a lookout, but Sam says theres no need to do that just yet. Then at last he tells them to start looking out and before long Rupert and Willie shout together, "There it is!" And there lies the island.

RUPERT MEETS THE CRAB

They waste no time, but head for shore;
All three are anxious to explore.

But when upon the shore they leap,
They find the cliffs are much too steep.

Sam says, "There'll be a path somewhere.
So I'll search this way, you look there."

They turn a corner, start in fear
To see a giant crab appear.

The island rises to a peak which towers over the little boat as it sails into the lagoon, a sheltered stretch of water between two arms of land. The peak is crowned by a pillar of rock. The three friends peer up at it from the beach and Sam, who has been studying the map, says, "If I know anything about pirates—which I do—then any treasure is somewhere near that rock pillar up there." But how to get to it, that is the problem, for the cliffs rise sheer from the beach. "We'll just have to split up and look for a path to the top," Sam decides. "You two go that way along the shore and I'll go the other. There's got to be a path to the top. All we've got to do is find it." So Rupert and Willie set off along the shore looking for any likely way to the top. Then as they pick their way among some boulders they hear a strange rattling, clacking sound and to their horror an absolutely huge crab appears.

RUPERT DISCOVERS A SIGN

The pals are stunned to hear it say,
"Do, please, let me show you the way."

"You'll be all right, although it's steep,
If to the narrow path you keep."

At length they reach the island's top,
So breathless, they just have to stop.

Then at a rocky pillar's base,
An arrow points straight up the face.

But in a moment the pals' horror turns to astonishment for the crab speaks, and very politely too. "May I help you, young sirs?" it asks. "W-we're looking for a way to the top of the island," Rupert stammers. "There is a way near here," says the crab. "It's steep and narrow but safe enough it you stick to the path. Come along." And soon, having thanked the crab, Rupert and Willie are toiling up a rocky cleft which seems to get steeper all the time. At last they come out on open rock but by now they are so hot and tired they just have to stop for a rest. Then on they go again, often on hands and knees because the rocks are so steep, until at last they find themselves at the base of the great pillar of rock. "Look!" exclaims Willie and points to something. It is an arrow made of old ship's timbers. And it is pointing to the top of the pillar. "Let's get Sam!" Rupert cries.

RUPERT FLIES A KITE

"Oh, Sam," they cry, "we have explored,
And may have traced the treasure hoard!"

They climb back up the rocky gap.
Sam says, "This pillar's on the map."

Says Rupert, "If you make a kite,
Then I can scale that rocky height."

Next on the kite some rope they tie,
And watch while Rupert makes it fly.

The pals race back to the beach and gasp out their story to Sam. "Soon as you've had a rest we'll go up again," Sam decides. But while they rest Rupert is thinking and at his suggestion they take back up with them two thin pieces of wood, a piece of sailcloth, some twine and a length of rope. As soon as Sam sees the wooden arrow he exclaims, "Pirate signpost! There's treasure up there all right. But how do we get up to it?" "Now that's why I asked you to bring up this sailcloth and stuff," Rupert says. "Sam, do you think you could make a kite?" "A kite?" Sam cries. "Easy!" And producing a sail-maker's needle from a pouch he sets to with the sticks, sailcloth and twine. In no time he has made a light, strong kite. The long rope is tied to the kite-string. Then Rupert takes it to the top of a nearby mound and launches it with the breeze. "Aha!" cries Sam, "I see now what he's trying to do!"

RUPERT FINDS THE TREASURE

Then when the kite comes tumbling down,
The rope hangs from the pillar's crown.

With Sam to keep the rope secure,
Rupert can reach the top, he's sure.

And there, before his very eyes,
A big, old wooden sea-chest lies!

The ancient rusted lock he hits;
The frail old sea-chest falls to bits.

At home on Nutwood common Rupert has often practised with his own kite. Skilfully he flies this one over the rock pillar, then at just the right moment sends it swooping to the ground so that its string is hanging over the top of the pillar. "Now all we have to do," Sam tells Willie, "is to pull the rope that's tied to the kite-string up and over the rock so that it hangs down both sides. Then we tie one end securely and someone climbs up the other." "And that better be me," Rupert volunteers. "I'm quite good at climbing." So while Sam holds it steady, Rupert shins up the rope. When at last he pulls himself on to the pillar's flat crown he lets out a great "Ah!" For there before him is an ancient iron-bound chest. He approaches slowly and examines it. The wood looks rotten and the lock rusted. He bangs the lock with his hand. And the chest falls to bits, spilling gold, silver and gems.

RUPERT SAILS FOR HOME

Now Rupert says, "The kite I'll drag
Up here and use it as a bag."

He lowers the treasure to his friends,
Then down the rope himself descends.

Amazed, the three friends stand and stare
At all the treasure they will share.

And now that their adventure's done,
They sail home in the setting sun.

"I've found it! I've found it!" Rupert calls down to the others. "How are you going to get it down?" Willie yells. "With the kite!" the little bear laughs. Then he pulls up the free end of the rope with the kite attached to it and strips the sailcloth from its frame of wood. Then he spreads it on the rock, fills it with the treasure, ties the corners together and lowers it to his friends. Then when the rope is secure again he climbs down.

On the beach the delighted friends stare in wonder at the treasure they have found. "I know," says Sam, "we'll keep just a little for ourselves and share the rest among any of our Nutwood people who are a bit short of money." Rupert and Willie think this is a grand idea. But later as they are sailing back to their own coast in the sunset Rupert says, "And I vote we keep something for Podgy. But for him we'd never have found the red box!"

Rupert's Memory Test

Try this memory test only when you have read all the stories in the book. Once you have read them look at the pictures below. Each is taken from a picture you will have seen in one or other of the stories. Then see if you can answer the questions at the bottom of the page. When you are done check the stories to see if you were right.

AND NOW DO YOU KNOW . . .

1. Who are the pals waiting for?
2. Mrs. Bear's umbrella is made of what?
3. What are these little men doing?
4. What did this machine show?
5. "Keep your eyes open . . ." For what?
6. Which tunnel is Rupert meant to take?
7. Who lives and works here?
8. What is special about this coal?

9. What does the crab show Rupert?
10. Why is Pong Ping sad?
11. What has upset Mrs. Sheep?
12. What comes in answer to this call?
13. What does the Conjurer's gadget show?
14. What is in this flask?
15. Why is this man surprised?
16. Who threw this snowball?